ABOUT THE AUTHOR:

Reed Duncan is an author as well as a former reading instructor, teacher, and school administrator. He lives in Vermont. The Rollo stories are based on Reed and his real-life, rambunctious bulldog who's very good at hiding, and is *always* hungry.

W

PENGUIN WORKSHOP
An Imprint of Penguin Random House LLC, New York

Text copyright © 2019 by Reed Duncan. Illustrations copyright © 2019 by Penguin Random House LLC. All rights reserved. Published by Penguin Workshop, an imprint of Penguin Random House LLC, New York. PENGUIN and PENGUIN WORKSHOP are trademarks of Penguin Books Ltd, and the W colophon is a registered trademark of Penguin Random House LLC. Manufactured in China.

Visit us online at www.penguinrandomhouse.com.

Library of Congress Cataloging-in-Publication Data is available upon request.

ISBN 9781524792466   10 9 8 7 6 5 4 3 2 1

WHERE'S ROLLO?

by REED DUNCAN
illustrated by KEITH FRAWLEY

PENGUIN WORKSHOP

Where's Rollo?
Is he hiding?

I have a treat for him.

Is Rollo upstairs?

I don't see him.

Is Rollo up in the attic?

He doesn't seem to be here.

Is Rollo downstairs in the dining room?

I don't see him anywhere.

I wonder if Rollo is hungry.

Maybe he's down in the basement?
He doesn't seem to be here, either.

I know!
Rollo must be outside.

I can't wait to give him his treat!

Is Rollo in the garden
or beyond the fence?

Is he behind a bush . . .

or in a tree?

Hmm . . . I don't see Rollo.
Where could he be?

Maybe Rollo *is* in the house.
Is he under the stairs?

I don't see Rollo anywhere.

Where's Rollo?

Will I ever find him?
Will he *ever* get his treat?

I know!

Maybe Rollo is sleeping.

Here he is.

I found you, Rollo.

Were you here the whole time . . . ?
You must be very hungry.

Would you like a treat, Rollo?